This book belongs to:

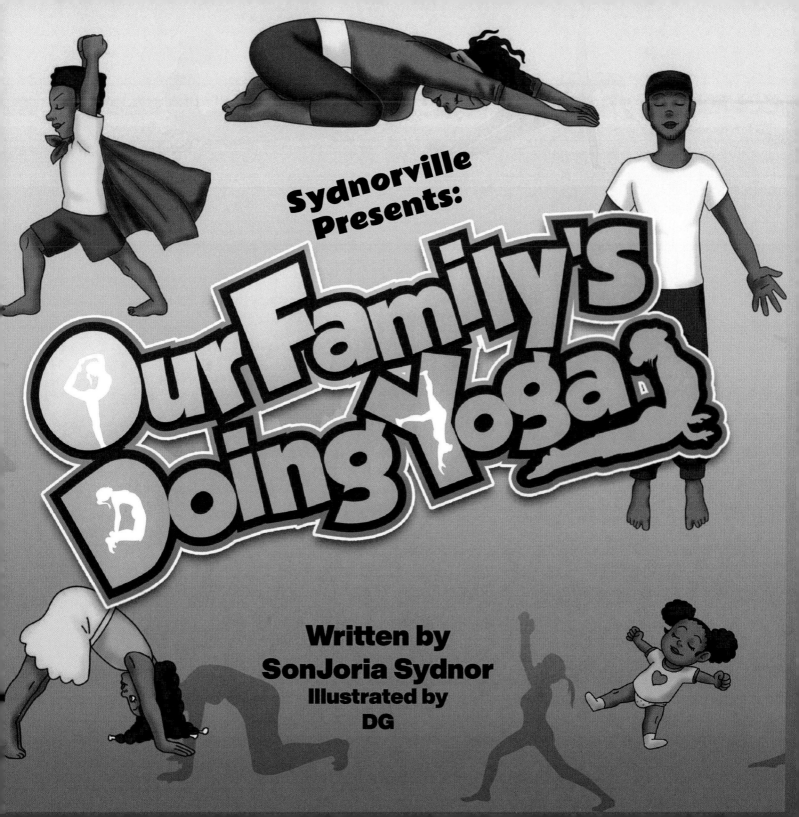

Sydnorville
Presents:

Our Family's Doing Yoga

Written by
SonJoria Sydnor
Illustrated by
DG

Published by SonJoria Sydnor
St. Louis, Missouri

Library of Congress Control Number: 2020908053

Printed in the United States of America

ISBN-13: ISBN 978-0-578-67635-7

Dedication

This book is dedicated to my Sydnorville: Jauron Sr., Jauron II, SonJaia and Sonaija, who "drove me" to my journey with yoga and joined me on my path.

We give kisses, hugs and snuggles.
Sometimes maybe there's a shove.

But our house is always lit!
Yeah, we know it's full of love.

1

All dressed in our favorite costumes.
Begging Mom to watch our show.

Learning so much, lots of questions.
Asking, "Mommy, did you know?"

2

Mama says, "Settle down, or
you're heading for a nap!"

4

We splatter paint and sprinkle glitter, bang on drums and bounce on balls.

While our mom is making dinner, the baby's drawing on the walls.

5

Seems like Mama's always cleaning.
Guess we really made a mess.

For us, it's a big adventure, but our
mom is looking stressed.

6

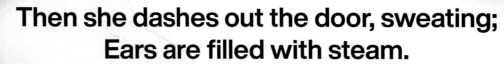

Then she dashes out the door, sweating;
Ears are filled with steam.

7

We're all gathered at the window—
our dog has caused a scene.

Daddy says she needs a break,
but I don't want our mom to leave.

So I tell her about mindfulness;
I learned about it on T.V.

I heard it helps to keep you calm,
kind of like a superpower.

You just focus on your breathing for
a minute or an hour.

10

We lay out our mats to join in, too.
This really worked out great.

Now our family's doing yoga,
and we even meditate.

11

First, we calm ourselves with feathers,
to begin our breathing flow.

Next, we stand tall like a mountain,
then lie down just like a bow.

12

Downward Dog pose is a favorite.
Seated Lotus keeps us tame.

13

But the giggles become louder when
we're practicing the Crane.

14

I never knew we'd enjoy Cobra,
head stands, Tree and lots of flopping.

17

18

19

Yoga, breath, and meditation.
Now our family time is popping!

I Spy YogaGame

There are yoga poses pictured throughout this book.
Read the description of poses below. With the help of an adult,
try out each pose. Afterwards reread and find the listed poses.

1. STAR POSE - Begin standing tall with both hands at your sides. Stretch your arms and legs out wide like a star.

2. DANCER'S POSE - Begin standing tall with both hands at your sides. Shift your weight to one foot. Bend the opposite knee, lifting feet off the floor, and reach your hands back to grab your lifted foot.

3. RESTING POSE - Begin on your back. Gently close your eyes with legs straight and arms at your sides.

4. SQUAT POSE - Begin standing tall. Step your legs out wider than your hips with your back straight. Begin to bend your knees and lower your tail bone towards the ground. Hands can be out like goalposts or together in prayer position.

5. HALF FORWARD FOLD - Begin standing tall, with a slight bend in your knees. Bend your head and chest towards the ground. Stop halfway. Place your hands on your thighs. Begin to straighten your legs and flatten your back like a table.

6. RUNNER'S LUNGE - Begin in a push-up/plank position, arms straight, legs extended back. Step your right foot forward next to your right pinky finger. Then try it on the left side.

7. CAT POSE - Begin on hands and knees. Bring your chin towards your chest and arch your back, pulling your belly in towards your back.

21

8. FROG POSE - Begin on hands and knees. Shift both knees out wider than your hips, lowering your belly to the floor. Lower your forearms to the floor, palms flat.

9. WARRIOR POSE - Begin standing tall, both feet hip-distance apart. Step one foot back, bending front knee. Reach hands for the sky. Repeat on opposite side.

10. BUTTERFLY POSE - Begin in a seated position. With a tall back, bring the bottoms of your feet together. Rest your hands on your knees.

11. MOUNTAIN POSE - Begin standing, hands at sides. Stand tall and strong.

12. BOW POSE - Begin lying on your belly. Bend your knees, bringing your heels towards your tail bone, and reach for your ankles.

13. DOWNWARD DOG POSE - Begin on hands and knees. Lift up on your toes, pushing your tail bone up and back towards the sky.

14. CHILD'S POSE - Begin on hands and knees. Bring your big toes together, sliding your knees wider than your hips. Sit your tail bone back to rest on your feet. Extend your arms out straight in front of you or rest them at your sides.

15. TREE POSE - Begin standing tall with both hands at your sides. Focus on a non-moving spot. Bring the bottom of one foot to the ankle, shin or thigh of the opposite leg. Hands can remain at your sides, extended up or together at prayer position. Repeat on opposite side.

16. COBRA POSE - Begin lying flat on your belly, legs and hands extended in front of you, palms of hands flat on your mat. Begin to bend your elbows, pulling them towards your sides. Press elbows towards your sides and slightly lift your chest off the floor.

I Spy YogaGame

1. Star Pose

2. Dancer's Pose

3. Resting Pose

4. Squat Pose

5. Half Forward Fold

6. Runner's Lunge

7. Cat Pose

8. Frog Pose

23

I Spy
Yoga Game

9. Warrior Pose **10. Butterfly Pose** **11. Mountain Pose** **12. Bow Pose**

13. Downward Dog Pose **14. Child's Pose** **15. Tree Pose** **16. Cobra Pose**

Sydnorville Favorites

Here are some of our favorite ways to practice yoga as a family. The key is to mix it up, trying new things and remember that yoga is more than just poses.

Yogi Says

The designated leader calls out a yoga pose. Participants follow the command but not without first hearing the key words "yogi says." If you get caught in a pose without having heard the magic words, you sit out. The last person standing wins. This game can also be played for fun without anyone sitting out.

Yoga Freeze Dance

Dance party! Turn on some fun tunes and get your jam on. When the designated leader stops the music and calls out a pose,

participants must freeze in the pose until the music starts again.

Flower Breathing

Using a flower or your finger slowly inhale through your nose smelling the flower and slowly exhale through the mouth blowing the petals. This is a great cue for children who need help calming through frustrations or fear.

Journaling

Designate a notebook as a journal. Sit down together and write or draw pictures. Use topics like "What does family mean to you?", "What do you feel grateful for?" or freestyle journaling about whatever comes to mind.

26

Author Insight

Yoga is an ancient practice from India and a great technique to connect the breath and body. Focusing on your breath, yoga draws your attention inward; it slows everyone down and brings you into the present moment. Because it teaches mindfulness and self-control, yoga makes for a great family activity. Enjoy reading this book, explore the poses together as a family and visit us on social media **@SydnorvilleBooks**. Leave a review of how *Our Family's Doing Yoga* helped build your yoga practice, and stay updated about upcoming events and the next book in the Sydnorville series.

About the Author

SonJoria Sydnor is a certified yoga instructor and educator with over 15 years of experience in early childhood education. As a wife and mother of three amazing children, her yoga practice naturally grew into an activity for the entire family.

When the Sydnors sought out a book to complement their new family pastime, they found many about yoga but none that focused on a black family, so SonJoria and her son decided to write their own. They are super excited to share the first book in Sydnorville!

28